OWL AND BILLY

OWL AND BILLY AND THE SPACE DAYS

MARTIN WADDELL

Illustrated by Carolyn Dinan

Specially produced by Mammoth for School Book Fairs

First published in Great Britain as two separate volumes:

Owl and Billy
First published in Great Britain 1986
by Methuen Children's Books Ltd
Published 1988 by Magnet
Text copyright © 1986 Martin Waddell
Illustrations copyright © 1986 Carolyn Dinan

Owl and Billy and the Space Days
First published in Great Britain 1988
by Methuen Children's Books Ltd
Published 1989 by Magnet
Text copyright © 1988 Martin Waddell
Illustrations copyright © 1988 Carolyn Dinan

This omnibus edition published 1991 specially for
School Book Fairs Ltd by Mammoth,
an imprint of Mandarin Paperbacks
Michelin House, 81 Fulham Road, London SW3 6RB

Mandarin is an imprint of the Octopus Publishing Group,
a division of Reed International Books Ltd

ISBN 0 7497 1116 7

A CIP catalogue record for this title
is available from the British Library

Printed in Great Britain
by Cox & Wyman Ltd, Reading, Berkshire

Contents

A book for Catriona

1. *The Secret Spaceman*

All the Big Ones in Speck Street went to school, but Billy Ogle couldn't go for another week because he was too small.

'I want to go to school *now*, Mum,' he told his mum.

'Next week, Billy,' said Mum. 'After your birthday.'

'I don't want to wait until next week,' said Billy.

'Well, you'll have to,' said Mum. 'Miss Murphy can't take you in Reception Class until after your birthday.'

Billy wasn't pleased.

'There's nobody left to play with except Wilkins' baby,' he said. 'Wilkins' baby doesn't go to school.'

Wilkins' baby was very small. Billy wheeled it sometimes with Mrs Wilkins, and he held the powder when she changed its nappy, but there wasn't much else he could do with it. It was a useless baby.

'I'm not going to play with Wilkins' baby,' Billy told his mum. 'I'm taking Owl for a ride instead.'

Owl was Billy's best friend. Billy's mum

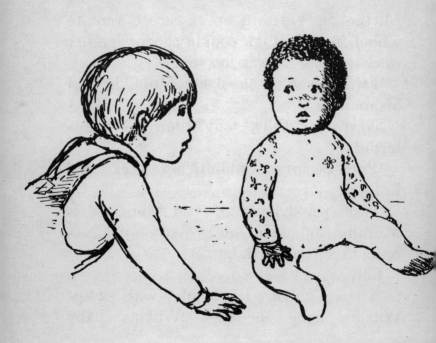

had made Owl out of an old pillowcase and some stuffing. Owl was good fun to play with.

Owl and Billy went down Speck Street. They didn't walk. They went on Billy's tricycle. Owl sat on the handlebars, but he nearly fell off in surprise when they saw the van outside the Old Folks.

It was a big green van, and some men were taking furniture out of it. They were moving the furniture into Mrs Bone's flat.

It was very old furniture, all wobbly-legged and patchy.

'I don't think Skinny Bone will be pleased,' Billy told the furniture man.

'Who?' said the man.

'Mrs Bone,' said Billy. 'Mrs Bone has furniture already. I don't think she will be pleased if you put all that stuff on top of it.'

Skinny Bone was a big fat lady. She chased people out of her garden. She was never pleased about anything.

'I dunno about that!' the man said, and he went on moving furniture. There was a hallstand with one peg missing, and a chair with broken springs, and an old cooker and . . .

'That's a *motorbike*!' gasped Billy.

Owl didn't know what a motorbike was, and Billy had to show him. It was a big black motorbike, with red demons painted on the side. It was too heavy to lift out of the van, and the furniture man had to put up a plank and wheel the motorbike down on to the road. Then the man put it in Skinny Bone's garden.

'Skinny Bone will start banging!' Billy told Owl.

Skinny Bone had a big stick and she banged it on the window when people went in her garden.

Owl told Billy he didn't like Skinny Bone when she banged.

'Mrs Bone's got a motorbike, Mum,' Billy told his mum, when they got home. He made a lot of Skinny-Bone-on-her-motorbike-riding-round-the-garden noises up and down the kitchen to show Mum what Skinny Bone on a motorbike would be like.

'Mrs Bone's gone,' said Mum.

'Gone?' said Billy.

'Not-Coming-Back-Gone-To-Australia-Gone,' said Mum.

'Did she forget her bike?' asked Billy.

'The bike belongs to someone else,' said Mum.

'What is it doing in Mrs Bone's garden if it belongs to someone else?' Billy asked.

'It isn't Mrs Bone's garden any more, Billy,' said Mum. 'Somebody new is coming to live in Mrs Bone's flat.'

'Somebody who rides a motorbike,' said

Billy.

There were six Old Folks' flats, with six Old Folks in them. They were built with the ordinary Speck Street houses around them so that the Old Folks would have people to play with. Most of the Old Folks weren't much good at playing. They sat about in their gardens and were cross, and none of them rode motorbikes.

'Owl wants to see the motorbike again,' Billy said, and Owl and Billy went off up Speck Street to see it.

'Stop,' said Billy. '*Look!*'

Owl looked, and nearly fell off the handlebars again.

'A *Spaceman!*' said Billy.

There was a Spaceman in Skinny Bone's flat. The Spaceman was dressed in black, and he had a big round space helmet on his head. He looked as if he had come down WHOOSH from Mars in a space rocket. Owl and Billy stood up on the wall of Skinny Bone's garden to get a better look.

The Spaceman saw them.

He looked at them through the window in his space helmet. Then he winked at Billy, and he raised his hand and waved. The hand was covered in a space glove, which was big and black and stretched halfway up his arm.

'Rubber arms!' gasped Billy, and Owl thought they were too.

'It might just be his space suit,' said Billy after a minute. 'And it *might* be rubber arms.'

Owl thought they should ask the Spaceman, but Billy couldn't, because he

wasn't allowed to speak to anyone Mum didn't know.

Owl and Billy went back home.

'There is a Spaceman in Mrs Bone's flat, with rubber arms,' Billy told his mum. 'Owl saw him.'

'Is there?' said Mum, in her I-don't-believe-Billy voice.

'Owl *says* he's a Spaceman,' said Billy. 'Owl *thinks* the Spaceman has rubber arms, but I think they might be part of his space suit.'

'What planet does he come from?' asked Mum, switching off the cleaner.

'Owl thinks Mars,' said Billy.

'What do *you* think?' said Mum.

'Venus!' said Billy, who knew all about planets because he had a book about them.

'Not Watford?' said Mum. 'That's what it said on the removal van. WATFORD in big red letters.'

'Owl says the Spaceman comes from trillions of light years away,' said Billy.

'Perhaps he stopped off at Watford on the way,' said Mum. 'Why don't you ask him?'

'Owl said not to speak to the Spaceman

14

because you didn't know him,' said Billy. 'Do you know the Spaceman, Mum?'

'Tell him Nora Wright sent you,' said Mum.

'Your name isn't Nora Wright,' Billy said.

'It isn't now,' said Mum. 'It used to be.'

'Is "Nora Wright" a sort of password, Mum?' Billy asked.

'That's right,' said Mum. 'You try it, and see what happens!'

Owl and Billy rode back to the Old Folks, on Billy's tricycle.

The Spaceman was standing in the garden, still wearing his space suit.

' "*Nora Wright sent us*," ' said Billy, and then he added, 'it's a sort of password.'

'I see,' said the Spaceman.

'This is Owl,' said Billy, showing Owl to the Spaceman. 'Owl thinks that you are a Spaceman.'

'How did he know?' asked the Spaceman.

'I told him that you had a space helmet,' said Billy. 'That's how he knew.'

'Well spotted!' said the Spaceman.

'Are you a *real* Spaceman?' Billy asked. 'A Spaceman from Watford?'

'That's right,' said the Spaceman. 'But don't tell! Nobody is supposed to know.'

'Except me and Owl,' said Billy.

'Correct,' said the Spaceman.

'And my mum,' said Billy.

'If you say so,' said the Spaceman. 'But absolutely *nobody* else!'

Then he got on to his motorbike and zoom-varoomed off down Speck Street, but before he went he hooted his horn three times.

'That must be a Space Signal!' Billy told Owl, and Owl said that proved the Spaceman was a spaceman.

'But we mustn't tell anyone,' Billy said, and Owl said he wouldn't.

2. *The Spaceman Pays a Visit*

Next day, when Billy was having his breakfast, there was a loud noise.

VAROOM!

VAROOM! VAROOM!

'What's that?' asked Billy's dad, and he went to look out of the window.

VAROOM!

VAROOM! VAROOM!

'Some old codger fiddling with a motorbike,' said Dad.

'Owl wants to know what a codger is, Dad,' said Billy.

'Somebody who is very old,' said Dad.

'Like you?' said Billy.

'No,' said Dad. 'Much older.'

'Like the Old Folks,' said Mum helpfully.

VAROOM!

VAROOM! VAROOM!

Billy didn't say anything, but he knew who the codger was. There was only one codger in Speck Street who went *Varoom*, and that was the Secret Spaceman.

'Wonder who he is?' Dad said. 'I haven't seen that one around before.'

'He's the one I told you about,' said Mum. 'He comes from Watford. Billy says he's a spaceman.'

'Does he?' said Dad.

Billy didn't say anything. He was cross, and so was Owl. The Spaceman was a Special Secret, not to be told to anyone, and anyone included Dad.

Billy waited until Dad had gone off to work, and then he was cross with Mum.

'You told on him!' he said.

'On who?' said Mum.

'The Spaceman,' said Billy.

'Oh dear,' said Mum.

'You weren't supposed to tell anyone that there was a Spaceman,' said Billy. 'Only you and me and Owl and the Spaceman know, and you are only in it because we told you accidentally, before we knew it was a Special Secret.'

'I don't suppose the Spaceman will mind your dad knowing,' said Mum.

'He minds very much,' said Billy. 'It is Top Secret Space Information.'

Owl said that it was too.

'Well, we won't tell your dad, then,' said Mum.

'You've already told him,' Billy said.

'I told him that there was a new tenant in the Old Folks and that I used to know him in Watford when I was little like you,' Mum said. 'I said that *you* said he was a spaceman, but your Dad thinks you are only making it up.'

'Owl says you'll have to promise not to tell again,' Billy said.

'Tell Owl I promise,' said Mum, and Owl said that was all right.

After breakfast Owl and Billy went for a ride on Billy's tricycle, and Owl wanted to visit the Spaceman, so they rang the Spaceman's doorbell.

'Who's that?' shouted a sleepy voice from inside the Spaceman's house.

'Owl and Billy,' said Billy.

The Spaceman opened the door.

He hadn't got his helmet on, that was the first thing Billy noticed; and the second was that the Spaceman hadn't got much hair. The top of his head was bald and shiny, like an apple, with little brown spots.

'You've got brown spots on your head,' Billy told the Spaceman.

'Space rays!' said the Spaceman.

'Did they burn all your hair off?' asked Billy.

'It isn't all off,' said the Spaceman.

'You haven't got very many hairs,' said Billy, and the Spaceman didn't look very pleased.

'Owl thought you might come out to play,' said Billy.

'Can't,' said the Spaceman.

'Why not?' asked Billy.

'Receiving messages,' said the Spaceman. 'Messages from Outer Space.'

'Oh,' said Billy.

Owl wanted to know what kind of messages, so Billy asked the Spaceman.

'Messages like "You've run out of milk", ' said the Spaceman.

'Have you?' said Billy.

'Yes,' said the Spaceman.

'I'll get some for you, if you like,' said Billy, and the Spaceman gave Billy milk money.

Owl and Billy went to Mrs Jefferson's shop
on the corner to get some, and they didn't
drop it on the way back.

'Thank you very much,' said the Spaceman, and he gave Billy 5p for not dropping
the milk.

Owl and Billy went home.

'Where have you been?' Mum asked.

'We were visiting the Spaceman,' Billy
said, and he showed Mum the 5p.

'Oh dear,' said Mum. 'You mustn't pester

him, Billy.'

'I'm not,' said Billy. 'I was helping.' And he told Mum about the Space-Message, and Not-Dropping-the-Milk.

'That was very good of you, Billy,' she said. 'But you musn't go knocking on the Old Folks' doors and disturbing them.'

'I only did it because Owl asked me to,' Billy said.

'Yes, *well*,' said Mum. 'That's all right, but you must tell Owl he isn't to go disturbing Mr Bennet again.'

'Who is Mr Bennet?' asked Billy. 'Is he my Spaceman?'

'Yes,' said Mum.

'Are you sure that's his name?' asked Billy, who thought that "Mr Bennet" was a funny name for a Spaceman.

'Yes,' said Mum.

'I'm going to ask him if it really is,' said Billy, hopping on his tricycle.

'Oh no you're not,' said Mum. 'You're going to help me with the dishes.'

Billy helped with the dishes and Owl watched, and then Owl decided that he wanted to go and play with the Spaceman.

24

'Later, Billy,' said Mum.

'Owl wants to go now,' said Billy.

'Owl can't,' said Mum. 'Mr Bennet is a very old man. I'm not sure that he wants to play with Owl all day.'

'Shall I go and ask him, Mum?' Billy asked.

'No,' said Mum.

Owl and Billy had to stay at home.

They stayed at home all morning and Billy played football with Owl. Owl wasn't much good at football and Billy won. Then they played races round the sitting room, and Billy won again. Then Wilkins' baby came to play for half an hour while Mrs Wilkins went off to the shops, and Mum read Owl and Billy and Wilkins' baby a story.

'Can Owl go and see the Spaceman now, Mum?' Billy asked.

'No, Billy,' said Mum.

Mrs Wilkins came back and had coffee with Mum, and she said, 'Soon be going to school, Billy, now you are a big boy.'

'Can't be too soon for Billy,' Mum said. 'He gets very bored playing by himself.'

'I play with Owl,' Billy said.

They had their dinner, and then Owl and Billy went for a tricycle ride, but the Spaceman wasn't there when they rode past his flat.

Owl wanted to ring the doorbell, in case the Spaceman was inside getting messages from Outer Space.

'Mum doesn't let us,' Billy told him. Instead they had races up and down the pavement outside the Spaceman's flat. But the Spaceman didn't come out.

They went home, and Billy read Owl the story Mum had read to Wilkins' baby. Billy knew nearly all the words.

Mum gave them biscuits, and Owl and Billy sat in the window and watched the Spaceman's garden, but the Spaceman didn't appear.

'Owl wants to go and see if the Spaceman's in his flat, Mum,' Billy said.

'Not just now, Billy,' said Mum. 'Come and help me with the hoover.'

'Owl doesn't want to,' Billy said.

'You *can* do things that Owl doesn't want to,' Mum said. 'Owl doesn't give you orders.'

'I don't want to either,' said Billy.

'Thanks for nothing!' Mum said, and she

went on hoovering.

Then ...

Brrrrrrrrrrrr! Brrrrrrrrr! Brrrrrrrr! went
the doorbell, three times.

Mum went to open the door. It was the
Spaceman.

'Hullo, Mr Bennet!' Mum said, and she
gave the Spaceman a big hug.

'Little Nora!' said the Spaceman.

'My mum isn't little!' said Billy, but nobody paid any attention to him. The Spaceman was giving Billy's mum her big hug back, and they started talking and talking and laughing.

'Hullo,' Billy said.

'Hullo, you!' said the Spaceman, unhugging Mum.

'Have you come to play with us?' Billy asked.

'Now, Billy ... ' Mum began.

'Yes,' said the Spaceman.

Billy and the Spaceman and Owl and Mum all sat down in the front room and played a guessing game, and then Billy showed the Spaceman his Woggly Man. The Spaceman made Woggly Man walk up and down on his knee and then Mum made some coffee. Afterwards Owl and Billy and Woggly Man and the Spaceman all went out into the back and Billy showed the Spaceman Owl's house, and how to stand on one leg.

The Spaceman said, 'I've trouble enough standing up on two!' and Mum laughed.

'Time I went home,' the Spaceman said.

'I want you to stay and play,' said Billy.
'Poor Billy is waiting to start school,' Mum
said. 'He has no-one to play with.'

29

'I haven't much time for playing,' said the Spaceman. 'But I tell you what. If Billy comes over to my house sometimes and gives three rings on the bell, he can help me with my work.'

'Space Messages?' gasped Billy.

'And other things,' said the Spaceman mysteriously. 'Come back with me now, and I'll show you.'

Owl and Billy went back with the Spaceman, to his flat, and the Spaceman showed them some Secret Space Signals like this:

     which means 'YES'

and this

     which means 'NO'

and this

     which means 'I WANT TO THINK ABOUT IT'.

They tried the signals out.

'Are you Billy?' the Spaceman asked, and

Billy went

'Do you go to school yet?' the Spaceman asked, and Billy went

'Are you going to school *soon?*' the Space-man asked, and Billy went

'Is Owl going too?' the Spaceman asked.

'I don't know,' Billy said. 'I don't know if Owls can go to school.'

'Then go   ' the Spaceman said. 'That means you want to think about it!'

And Billy did.

When he got home, he asked Mum if Owl could go to school.

'I don't think there are many Owls in school, Billy,' Mum said. 'But I expect the teacher won't mind if you take Owl for the first few days.'

'Owl isn't sure if he wants to go to school, Mum,' Billy said. 'He says we have the Spaceman to play with, and we don't need to go to school now.'

31

'Owl's silly,' said Mum. 'You tell him how nice school is.'

'I don't know how nice it is,' said Billy.

'*Very* nice!' said Mum. 'You'll really like it, Billy. Don't worry.'

'I'm not,' said Billy. 'It was Owl who was worrying.'

'Tomorrow you can go and play with the Spaceman again, Billy,' said Mum. 'Stop worrying about old school, and think about that.'

Owl and Billy went upstairs to bed, and Owl asked Billy a lot of questions and Billy

told him the answers using the Spaceman's Secret Signals. It was great fun, and Billy forgot all about going to school.

So did Owl.

3. *Billy and the Secret Messages*

'Mum?' said Billy the next morning. 'Mum, what *is* Watford?'

'It's a place, Billy. I used to live there, before I met your dad.'

'*Before?*' asked Billy.

'We weren't always *Mum* and *Dad*, Billy,' said Mum. 'I was a little girl and he was a little boy like you, and we grew up, and we met, and then we had a little boy of our own, called Billy.'

'That's me,' said Billy.

'Right,' said Mum.

'And then you made Owl,' said Billy.

'Exactly,' said Mum.

VAROOM!
VAROOM! VAROOM!

'There goes Mr Bennet again!' said Mum. 'Go and tell him he's making a lot of noise.'

'All right,' said Billy, and he got out his tricycle and took Owl down to the Old Folks, where the Spaceman was varooming his motorbike.

'My mum says that you are making a lot of noise,' Billy told the Spaceman.

'I know,' said the Spaceman. He was lying on his back fiddling with some of the twiddly bits underneath his motorbike.

'Are you *really* called Mr Bennet?' Billy asked.

'That's what people call me,' said the Spaceman mysteriously.

Owl wanted to know what the Spaceman's real name was, so Billy asked him.

'Ah,' said the Spaceman.

'"Ah"?' said Billy. '"Ah" is a funny name.' Billy laughed at the funny name, and Owl did too.

'I didn't mean that "Ah" was my name,' said the Spaceman. 'I meant a That-Would-Be-Telling-Ah.'

Then he got up and sat on his motorbike, and tried the accelerator.

VAROOM! VAROOM!

'Fixed!' he said.

'Don't varoom it again, please,' Billy said. 'Owl's afraid that all the Old Folk will be

complaining.'

'I don't see anybody complaining,' said the Spaceman.

'There's old Pinball,' said Billy. 'He is the one who sticks pins in footballs. Miss Henshawe is the one with the smelly cat and Miss Rice has no teeth and Henny Compton has no legs.'

'No legs?' said the Spaceman.

'He has legs, sort of,' said Billy. 'They don't work properly. He's got a wheelchair. He's nice.'

'I *have* come down to a funny planet!' said the Spaceman.

They went into the Spaceman's flat, and he flopped down in his armchair and closed his eyes.

'Are you going to sleep?' Billy asked.

'No,' said the Spaceman. 'I'm receiving messages.'

'Oh,' said Billy. 'Can I do it?'

'No,' said the Spaceman. 'What you can do is to keep very still until I open my eyes again, and then I'll tell you what the message is.'

'Right,' said Billy, and he kept very still, until he had counted up to five three times.

37

'I'm going to count to ten when I go to school,' he told the Spaceman.

'Do five again,' said the Spaceman. 'The message is just coming through.'

Billy counted ONE-TWO-THREE-FOUR-FIVE again, and then Owl did it twice, and then Owl wouldn't do it any more.

'Owl is tired of counting,' Billy said.

'That's all right,' said the Spaceman. 'I've got the message now.'

'What message?' asked Billy.

'The message is: THERE IS ICE CREAM IN THE FRIDGE,' said the Spaceman.

'Is there?' said Billy.

'Well, there *wasn't*,' said the Spaceman. 'But if the message says there is now, I suppose there must be. Let's go and see.'

There was.

It was raspberry. Billy liked it, and Owl liked it, although he gave most of his to Billy.

'How did the ice cream get in the fridge?' Billy asked.

'Beamed down,' said the Spaceman. 'One minute it isn't there, and the next it just appears.'

'Could you beam down some more?' asked
Billy.

'Not today,' said the Spaceman.

'Could I be a Spaceman?'

'No,' said the Spaceman. 'You belong
down here. But you can be a Spaceman's

Assistant, and help me.'

'Good,' said Billy.

'Wait,' said the Spaceman. 'I'm getting *another* message.' He closed his eyes, and lay back in the chair.

'And ...

      the ...

            message ...

                 is ...

IT IS TIME FOR OWL AND BILLY TO GO HOME NOW.'

Billy thought about the Secret Message, and he asked Owl about it. Owl wasn't pleased.

'Owl doesn't want to go home,' Billy told the Spaceman.

'Then he won't find out *why*,' said the Spaceman.

'Why what?'

'Why it is time for you to go home,' said the Spaceman.

'I thought it was because you felt sleepy,' said Billy.

'There's another reason,' said the Spaceman. 'You ask your mother about it. She'll know what it is.'

Billy asked his mum when he got home.

'Quite right!' said Mum. 'There is a reason!'

'Oh,' said Billy. 'What is it?'

'*Because* ... because your new schoolbag has just come,' said Mum.

'OOOOOH!' said Billy.

It was a brilliant new schoolbag, and Owl fitted into it as well. It was brown, with straps

that went over Billy's shoulders, and buckles that Mum showed him how to work.

'I'm going to take it to show the Spaceman, Mum,' Billy said.

'No, Billy,' said Mum. 'I'm sure the Spaceman needs a long, long nap after all those messages.'

'They were TRUE too!' Billy said. 'There *was* ice cream in the fridge, and it *was* time I came home, because my schoolbag was here!'

'I think your Spaceman is very clever, Billy,' said Mum.

'I think so too,' said Billy.

And Owl thought that they were right.

4.   *Owl Runs Away*

'Today's a very important day!' Billy told the Spaceman on Thursday morning.

'Why?' said the Spaceman.

They were on their way back from Mrs Jefferson's shop on the corner where the Spaceman had been buying some very special tobacco for sending smoke signals.

'I'm going to see my new school,' said Billy.

'I see,' said the Spaceman.

'Did *you* go to school?' Billy asked, because he wasn't certain if Spacemen went to school.

'Yes,' said the Spaceman, and he gave Billy one of the Fizz Bombs he'd bought when he was getting the smoke-signal tobacco.

43

'Where was your school?' said Billy.
'Mine's on the Newton Road.'
'Mars,' said the Spaceman.

44

'Owl says he doesn't like my new school,' Billy said.

'But you will,' said the Spaceman.

'How do you know I will?' asked Billy.

'Got a message about it,' said the Spaceman. 'It said:

BILLY WILL LIKE SCHOOL.'

'Oh,' said Billy.

He told his mum about it on the way to see his new school that afternoon.

'I'm not surprised,' said Mum. 'It's a very nice school.'

'I know it is,' said Billy. 'But Owl doesn't like it.'

'Owl hasn't seen it yet,' said Mum, as they turned in the gate.

Billy took Owl out of his schoolbag, so that he could see what the new school was like.

Billy's new school wasn't new, it was old. It was made of red bricks, and it had two chimneys, and a door with a hall where Billy could hang his coat. Miss Murphy showed him where his coat would go, and she wrote out a label:

BILLY OGLE

45

Billy stuck the label above the coat-peg which was just beside the door of the classroom.

There was a sandpit and paint boards and cushions and desks and a water-play and a

46

slide and a little tiny garden with things growing in it.

'This is where you'll sit, Billy,' said Miss Murphy.

Owl and Billy sat down.

47

'Who is this you've brought with you?' Miss Murphy asked.

'Owl,' said Billy. 'I'm going to marry Owl when I grow up.'

'What does Owl think about that?' Miss Murphy asked.

'Owl's going to marry me too,' said Billy. 'Then we'll belong to each other.'

'I hope I'm invited to the wedding,' said Miss Murphy.

'We're inviting our friends,' said Billy, who wasn't very certain what a wedding was, but thought it was probably something like a birthday.

'It's my birthday soon,' Billy told Miss Murphy.

'Sunday,' said Mum.

'I'm having a party,' said Billy, but he didn't say anything about inviting Miss Murphy to it, because he wasn't certain if she was one of his friends.

Then they saw the playground, and the dining room where Billy would have his lunch, and they looked at the pictures on the walls, and then Miss Murphy said, 'Bye Bye, Billy, see you on Monday morning.'

Billy and Mum walked home.

'Your new school is nice, Billy,' Mum said.
'Lots of things to play with.'

'Y-e-s,' said Billy.

'And there'll be lots of children too. Boys

and girls.'

'Where were they?' Billy asked.

'They'd all gone home,' Mum said. 'We came down after school, so that you could see it.'

'Did they all go home because they didn't like it?' Billy asked.

'They all went home because it was time to go home,' said Mum. 'Everybody goes home after school.'

Billy thought about it. It was a long, long way to school from his house, and a long, long way back.

'I'm not sure I could *find* it,' he said uneasily.

'I'll take you there,' said Mum.

'And bring me back?' asked Billy.

'Every day,' said Mum.

'Every *single* day?' said Billy, who didn't at all like the idea of going to school every single day.

'Except Saturdays and Sundays,' said Mum. 'And there are holidays as well. Weeks and weeks of days when you don't go to school at all.'

When they got home, Billy went to tell the

Spaceman about it.

'Well?' said the Spaceman. 'Was my message right?'

'Y-e-s,' said Billy.

'My Space Messages are always right,' the Spaceman said.

'Owl didn't like it one bit,' said Billy.

'What didn't he like?' said the Spaceman.

'School,' said Billy.

'I'll have to speak to Owl about that,' said the Spaceman. 'Where is he, anyway?'

'In my schoolbag,' said Billy, and he opened his schoolbag to take Owl out of it but

OWL

WASN'T

THERE!

'What's the matter?' said the Spaceman.

'Owl's gone!' said Billy, holding his schoolbag open.

'I expect you left him at home,' said the Spaceman.

'I didn't,' said Billy.

'Perhaps your mum has him?' said the Spaceman.

'No she hasn't,' said Billy.

They went to Billy's house.

'Owl?' said Mum. 'Didn't you bring him home, Billy?'

Billy shook his head.

'Perhaps he dropped out on the way?' said the Spaceman.

'He's run away!' said Billy, feeling tears well up in his eyes.

'No he hasn't,' said Mum.

'Of course he hasn't,' said the Spaceman. 'Hang on a bit, and I'll go and look for him!'

The Spaceman went back to the Old Folks and put on his Spacesuit and the next thing Billy saw was him zoom-varooming off down the road on his motorbike.

'Here's Woggly Man come to see you,' Billy's mum said, and she gave Billy Woggly Man, but Billy didn't want Woggly Man, and he threw Woggly Man over the sofa.

'I'm sure Owl will turn up, Billy,' Mum said.

'He's run away,' Billy said.

'No he hasn't.'

'He's run away because he didn't like school,' said Billy. 'He didn't like Miss Murphy and he doesn't want to go there every day.'

Mum made Billy an orange drink, and gave him some biscuits, but Billy didn't eat any. He didn't feel like biscuits. He wanted Owl.

Then . . .

Zoom Varoom

The Spaceman's motorbike came whizzing down the road, and pulled up in front of Billy's house.

Billy ran to the door to let him in.

'Have you got Owl?' he asked.

'No,' said the Spaceman. 'No. I haven't got him, BUT...'

'But what?' asked Billy.

'BUT I got a message,' said the Spaceman.

'A Space Message?' asked Billy hopefully. 'A Space Message about Owl?'

'Right,' said the Spaceman. 'I got a Space Message saying:

OWL IS ALL RIGHT AND HE'LL BE HERE IN A MINUTE.'

'I hope you're right,' said Billy's mum. 'Are you certain this Space Message is going to work, Mr Bennet?'

'Spaceman's Honour,' said the Spaceman,

and he crossed his thumbs, like this

'Is that one of your secret signs?' Billy asked.

The Spaceman didn't say anything, but he

went which is the Secret Sign for 'Yes'.

'What's this all about?' asked Mum.

'It's Top Secret Space Information, Mum,'

55

said Billy. 'You're not allowed to know.'

Then . . .

BRRRRRNNNGGG

BRRRRRNNNGGG!

went the doorbell.

'Better go and see who that is, Billy,' said the Spaceman.

Billy opened the door, and it was his new teacher, Miss Murphy and . . .

OWL!

'Owl came back to school to see me, Billy,' Miss Murphy said. 'He wanted to be absolutely certain that you'd be all right, and I told him you would be. Now I've brought him back.'

Billy took Owl from her.

'Say thank you to Miss Murphy, Billy,' said Mum.

'Thank you, Miss Murphy,' said Billy, uncertainly.

Then Mum thanked Miss Murphy and the Spaceman thanked Miss Murphy and they went out to the door to see Miss Murphy off in her car.

Billy stayed on the sofa with Owl.

Mum came back into the house, and closed

56

the door behind her.

'Don't you go leaving Owl behind you again Billy!' she said. 'You're getting to be a big boy. You've got to learn to look after things.'

Billy cuddled Owl.

'Cheer up,' Mum said.

'Owl can't talk, Mum,' Billy said.

'You're always telling me he can,' said Mum.

'Only to me,' said Billy.

'So?' said Mum.

'Not Miss Murphy.'

'Miss Murphy was very kind coming all this distance out of her way to bring Owl back to you, Billy,' said Mum.

'Owl doesn't like her,' said Billy. 'Owl doesn't talk to her.'

'Tell Owl. . . .' Mum began, and then she said. 'Oh I don't know what you tell Owl. I get fed up with Owl sometimes.'

And she went out of the room.

That night, when Billy was getting tucked up in bed, he said, 'Mum!'

'Yes, Billy?'

'Owl isn't real, Mum. Owl's made of a

pillowcase, isn't he?'

'Yes, Billy,' said Mum.

'So he couldn't talk to Miss Murphy, could he? He only talks to me, because I'm the one you made him for.'

'I *suppose* that's right,' said Mum.

Billy thought about it.

'Miss Murphy tells lies, Mum,' he said. 'Miss Murphy said Owl talked to her, and he

58

didn't, because he's made of a pillowcase and he only talks to me.'

'Maybe Owl *did* tell her something, Billy,' Mum said.

'How?' Billy demanded.

'I don't know,' said Mum. 'Maybe some magic way. I think Owl told her you thought you might not like school either, and you were worried about it. And I think she brought Owl back here specially so he could tell you not to worry, because Miss Murphy is your friend.'

'Is she?' asked Billy.

'I think so,' said Mum. 'Why don't we ask Owl?'

And they did.

And Owl whispered something back to Billy, but Mum didn't know what it was,

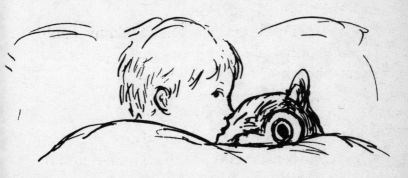

because only Billy could hear it.

'Well?' Mum said.

'Owl says Miss Murphy is my friend, Mum,' said Billy.

'I thought he would,' said Mum.

5. *Billy's Birthday*

Billy woke up very early on Sunday morning, because it was his birthday.

Nobody else was awake, not even Owl. Billy had to wake Owl up to tell him, and Owl was very pleased, because he had been waiting for Billy's birthday for a long time.

Owl and Billy went down to tell Billy's mum and dad.

'Huh? Wassat?' Billy's dad said, peering out from under the bedclothes.

'My birthday!' said Billy.

'Oooo-aaah!' groaned Dad, and he yawned sleepily.

'Happy Birthday to me!' said Billy, and Dad picked him from beside the bed and

snuggled him in beside Mum.

'Happy Birthday, Billy,' Mum whispered sleepily. 'Now go back to sleep.'

Billy couldn't get back to sleep, but he tried. He tried very hard, but Owl didn't try. Owl was too excited.

Owl wanted to play.

Owl played pulling the bedclothes, and then he played walking up Billy, and then he played walking up Mum, and then he played tickling Dad.

'Okay!' said Dad. 'I surrender!' and he got out of bed.

'What time is it?' muttered Mum.

'Six o' clock,' said Dad. 'Come on. We may as well pretend to be awake even if we aren't. You get the tea, and I'll get Billy's presents.'

'*You* get the tea,' said Mum. '*I'll* get Billy's presents!'

Billy got lots of presents.

There was a Big Space Lego set from Mum and a trumpet from Dad and a new coat from Aunt Paula and a Twisty Game from Uncle

James and a boiled egg with a face on from Woggly Man and a new jersey from the Wilkins and some sweets from Wilkins' baby and a toffee apple from Owl.

'Whose idea was that?' Mum said.

'Owl's, of course,' said Dad. 'With a little help from me.'

'Don't eat it in bed, Billy!' warned Mum. 'You'll get the bedclothes sticky.'

Billy went downstairs and ate Owl's toffee apple on the sofa, while he was playing the Twisty Game.

Then the postman came.

There was a Happy Birthday card from Mum and Dad and Owl and Woggly Man and another from the Wilkins. There was one from Miss Murphy at the school, and there was a card from Henny Compton, with 50p taped inside.

'You'll have to go across and thank Henny for it, Billy,' Mum said.

And then she sat down on the sofa, where she stuck.

'What am I sticking to?' she demanded.

'Owl thinks it *might* be toffee apple,' Billy said.

'Get your father!' Mum said. 'He brought it into the house, he can clean it off the sofa!'

'It wasn't Dad who got me the toffee apple, Mum,' said Billy. 'It was Owl.'

'Can Owl clean sofas?' Mum asked.

'No,' said Billy.

'Then get your father!' said Mum.

Dad started cleaning the sofa, and Mum went upstairs to clean her dress and Owl and Billy went across the road to say thank you to Henny Compton for the 50p.

'Hullo,' Henny said, drawing his wheelchair back from the door to let Billy in.

'Hullo,' said Billy. 'Mum said I was to Thank-You-For-The-50p-And-The-Lovely-Card and you can come to my party this afternoon, if you want to. It's at three o'clock and there's jelly.'

'I like jelly,' said Henny.

'If you're coming, bring your wheelchair,' said Billy.

'I'll have to,' said Henny.

'Good,' said Billy. 'I have a friend who doesn't know about wheelchairs. I want him to see it.'

'Who?' said Henny.

'The Spa.... ' began Billy, and then he stopped and said, 'Mr *Bennet*,' because the Spaceman was Top Secret Space Information, that Henny wasn't allowed to know about it.

'Owl wants to see it too,' Billy added.

'Owl's seen it before,' Henny said. Henny knew Owl well. Owl had been for rides in his wheelchair.

'He wants to see it *again*,' said Billy.

Then Billy went home.

It was a great Birthday Party.

Wilkins' baby was sick all over the carpet and Dad burnt himself lighting the birthday candles and Mrs Wilkins got toffee apple on her skirt. (It couldn't have come from the sofa because Dad had cleaned it.) Henny's wheelchair went over Auntie Paula's foot and Auntie Paula was very rude and Billy and Owl and Woggly Man laughed and Mum said they shouldn't.

The best bit was the Spaceman.

The Spaceman brought Billy a Special Spacesuit made of shiny stuff. It had a belt and badge and a space helmet and a ray gun.

'Do you like it, Billy?' the Spaceman asked,

and Billy went

Billy ray gunned Wilkins' baby and Mrs Wilkins and Mum and Dad and Woggly Man and Owl and Henny Compton's wheelchair and the jelly and the orangeade and the sandwiches and the little cakes with hats on.

'Don't ray gun me, Billy,' warned the Spaceman, and Billy went

Then they had their tea, and Wilkins' baby and Mrs Wilkins and Henny Compton went home, and then it was time to go to bed.

'I want the Spaceman to put me to bed, Mum,' Billy said, and the Spaceman did. Billy got up on the Spaceman's shoulders and they zoomed up the stairs like a space rocket, and then they had to zoom down again to get Owl.

'What about Woggly Man?' said Mum.

'Woggly Man doesn't sleep in my bed any more,' said Billy, but the Spaceman carried Woggly Man upstairs as well.

'Poor Woggly Man,' said the Spaceman, putting Woggly Man into the playbox. 'I hope you aren't lonely in there.'

'Owl says he isn't,' said Billy.

68

'How does Owl know?' said the Spaceman. 'Owl isn't lonely. Owl is in a nice comfy bed with you, not all alone in a playbox.'

'Owl knows,' said Billy.

'Owl doesn't know everything, Billy,' said the Spaceman, sitting down on the end of the bed. 'Lots of people get lonely.'

'Like old Henny?' said Billy.

'Not just old people, Billy,' said the Spaceman. 'Think about it!'

And Billy made the secret sign

The Spaceman went away, and Mum came up to tuck Billy in.

'Mum,' said Billy. 'Is the Spaceman lonely sometimes?'

'I expect he is, Billy,' said Mum.

'Like Woggly Man,' said Billy. 'Woggly Man is lonely, because Owl said there wasn't room for him in my bed.'

'Owl's wrong!' said Mum. 'There's plenty of room. Get Owl to move over!'

Billy moved Owl over, and Woggly Man got in.

69

'Now he won't be lonely, will he?' said Mum.

'Not a bit!' said Billy.

6. *Billy and the Monster*

It was Sunday afternoon, the Sunday before Going-to-School-Monday.

'Nice new clothes for going to school, Billy!' Mum said.

The new clothes were all laid out on the bed. There were two pairs of trousers, and two shirts, and two jerseys.

'You'll look great in them, Billy,' said Mum.

Billy looked at them.

'Owl says I'll be roasted if I have to wear *two* of everything,' he said.

'Then Owl is very silly!' said Mum. 'You only wear one pair of trousers, and one jersey, and one shirt at a time, the rest are spares.'

And she put Billy's new clothes on him.

Billy went downstairs and showed Dad, and then Owl said that they should go and show the Spaceman, and Mum said they could.

Owl and Billy went to the Spaceman's house and rang three times on the bell, because that was another kind of Secret Signal to let the Spaceman know who was at the door before he came to answer it.

'These are my new clothes for going to school in,' Billy told the Spaceman. 'Owl doesn't like them.'

'I think Owl is jealous,' said the Spaceman.

'Owl likes my spacesuit better,' said Billy. 'The one you gave me for my birthday. It has a ray gun. If I'd had my ray gun with me I could have shot the Monster in the hall.'

'What monster?' said the Spaceman.

'Owl says there was a Space Monster in the hall, outside your door,' said Billy. 'I could have shot him with my ray gun!'

'What was he like?' asked the Spaceman.

'Big,' said Billy. 'And hairy and nasty!'

'Where did he go?' asked the Spaceman. 'He isn't still there, is he?'

'I don't know,' said Billy.

They looked out in the hall, but the big hairy nasty Space Monster wasn't there.

'Spacesuits are for fighting Space Monsters in,' Billy said. 'I would have fought him if I'd had my spacesuit on. Spacesuits are for adventures.'

'Like your new clothes,' said the Spaceman.

'My new clothes are for going to school,' Billy said.

'Going to school is an adventure,' said the Spaceman.

'I bet there aren't any Space Monsters there!' said Billy.

'You never know with Space Monsters,' said the Spaceman.

Billy went home.

'Early bed, Billy,' said Mum, after tea. 'Big day tomorrow.'

'New school,' said Dad.

Billy didn't say anything.

He went upstairs with Mum and had a Special Bath with Mum's smelly soap, and Owl fell in.

Owl got wet, but he didn't drown because
Billy saved him. Billy was afraid that Owl
would catch cold but Mum said he wouldn't.
She dried Owl with the hairdryer while Dad

was reading Billy his story.

Billy and Owl and Woggly Man got into bed, though Owl had to stay on a towel down at the far end because he was still damp.

Mum gave Owl a Special Kiss to make up for it, and Billy and Woggly Man got one too.

'Keep the light on, Mum,' Billy said, and Mum said she would.

Billy couldn't get to sleep. He had to go downstairs to get a drink for Woggly Man and then he had to go down again to get something to keep Owl warm and then he left his ray gun behind, and he had to go down for it.

'What do you want your ray gun for, Billy?' Dad asked.

'The Monster,' said Billy.

'What Monster?'

'There's a big hairy nasty Space Monster!' Billy said.

'No there isn't,' said Dad.

'Yes there is,' said Billy. 'The Spa ... Mr Bennet knows all about it!'

Dad told Mum.

'You're not afraid of a silly Space Monster, Billy!' Mum said.

'Owl's afraid of it,' said Billy. 'And it isn't silly. I saw it at the Spaceman's.'

'I'll have to talk to the Spaceman about this, Billy,' said Mum, and she went straight over to the Spaceman's flat and came back with him.

'Hullo, Billy,' said the Spaceman. 'What's all this about a Monster?'

Billy didn't say anything. He just held on to Owl, because Owl was frightened of the Space Monster.

'I think maybe Owl *imagined* the Space Monster, Billy,' said Mum.

'No he didn't,' said Billy.

'What was this Monster like, Billy?' the Spaceman said.

'Big and hairy and nasty,' said Billy.

'How *nasty*?' said the Spaceman.

'Black teeth and red eyes!' said Billy.

'Oh,' said the Spaceman. 'That's all right then.'

'Why?' said Billy.

'It's a Go-Away Monster,' said the Space-man.

'Go-Away?' said Billy.

'Yes,' said the Spaceman. 'You just look at it and then you make a Secret Signal like this and it goes away!'

'Are you sure?' said Billy.

'Certain sure!' said the Spaceman. 'Those Go-Away Monsters are real scaredy custards!'

'I'm not,' said Billy. 'I'm brave.'

'Owl was the one who was frightened,' said Mum. 'Isn't that right, Billy?'

'Yes,' said Billy.

'You tell Owl not to be frightened any more, Billy,' said the Spaceman, and he went home.

'Mum,' said Billy, when Mum was putting him to bed. 'Mum, is Mr Bennet a Spaceman really?'

'I'm sure I don't know, Billy,' said Mum. 'What do you think?'

'Owl thinks he *might* be making it up,' said Billy. 'But I think he's a Spaceman.'

'I like him either way,' said Mum.

'So do I,' said Billy.

7. *Billy Goes to School*

Monday was Going-to-School-Day.

Mum and Billy and Owl went off to school, leaving Woggly Man at home, all alone.

'Woggly Man wants to come too, Mum,' Billy said. 'Owl told me so. Can I bring him?'

'No,' said Mum. 'Only Owl!'

'Why?'

'There wouldn't be room in school if the children brought all their friends with them,' said Mum.

Billy and Owl waved to Woggly Man who was sitting in the front room window where he could see them.

'Can I show the Spaceman my new school shoes?' Billy asked, when they were passing the Spaceman's flat, but Mum said the Spaceman wouldn't be up yet.

They went to school.

There were lots of children at school, and most of them were bigger than Billy, but he didn't mind because Mum came in with him, and helped him to hang up his coat on the peg where his name was.

Then Miss Murphy came.

She was very nice. She took Owl and Billy to Billy's special seat and they made another special seat for Owl, on a cushion.

There were other new children, just like Billy. Some of them were fat and some of them were thin and one of them had red trousers. His name was Sam. He sat next to Billy, and Owl didn't like him.

'This is Ann, Billy,' said Miss Murphy. 'Ann's going to show you and Sam all the things we do.'

Ann did.

There were lots of things to do.

Billy and Ann and Sam played with the water-tray, and then they worked with the sand, and then they sat down and had their rest, and then Miss Murphy read a story, and

then there were bricks, and then it was break.

'Will Mum come now?' Billy asked Miss Murphy.

'Not now,' said Miss Murphy. 'Later.' And then she helped Billy and Sam and Ann to dress up, and they went in the little house

with the blue door, and Billy and Sam made
tea while Ann was out working.

Ann got Billy some cars from the car box,

and they put them on Miss Murphy's road,
which ran over two whole tables, and they
went round and round the roads. Then they

had another story, and a song, and then they had dinner in the Little Ones' Dining Room. After that they went out to play and then they went in again and Miss Murphy talked a lot, and then it was time to go home.

'Where's Mum?' said Billy.

Mum came through the door. She was the first in of all the Mums and Dads and she met Ann and Sam.

'Sam's my best friend,' said Billy, when they got outside.

'Good,' said Mum.

'Ann's my next best!' said Billy.

'She looks nice,' said Mum.

'Mary Rowen fell in the mud,' said Billy, but Mum wasn't paying any attention. She was looking for something.

'I think you've forgotten something, Billy,' she said.

'No I haven't,' said Billy, because he knew he had his shoebag hanging up on its peg and his schoolbag on his back, with his pencils in it.

'Yes you have,' said Mum. 'You've forgotten Owl!'

They had to go all the way back into School

to get Owl, who'd moved up on to Miss Murphy's desk where he was waiting for Billy.

They went home and Billy had a warm drink and then the Spaceman came.

'Hullo, Billy,' he said. 'How's school?'

'Great,' said Billy, because it was, and he told the Spaceman all about Sam and Ann and Mary Rowen falling in the mud and what the Little Ones' Dining Room was like and what he had for dinner.

'What did Owl think?' the Spaceman said.

Billy thought a bit. 'Owl didn't like it very much,' he said.

'Oh dear,' said Mum. 'Why not?'

'Owl had no-one to play with,' said Billy.

'I thought he played with you?' said the Spaceman.

'I was *busy*,' Billy said. 'You have to be busy at school learning useful things.'

'I see,' said the Spaceman. And then he closed his eyes and had a Space Message. It said:

THERE'S A SURPRISE UNDER THE CUSHION.

And there was!

It was a bag of sweets.

'Not more sweets!' said Mum.

'Sweets for Owl!' said the Spaceman. 'I bet Owl could do with some, because he's had nobody to talk to all day, like me! I'm really missing Billy's visits, now he's gone to school.'

'I'll come and see you every day!' Billy said.

'Thank you very much,' said the Spaceman, and he went home.

Dad came home and Billy told him all about school and then they had their tea and then Dad read him a story and then Owl and Billy went up to bed, and Mum brought Woggly Man up afterwards.

'Here's poor old Woggly Man, Billy,' she said. 'He's been very lonely all day, and he thinks you've forgotten him.'

She put Woggly Man in bed, beside Billy and Owl.

'Owl was lonely too,' said Billy, 'because I was too busy to play with him.'

'I expect he was,' said Mum. 'There isn't really much for Owl to do at school, is there? I think he should stay at home tomorrow, and keep Woggly Man company. Then they could play with each other.'

Billy asked Owl, and Owl said it was a very good idea, and Woggly Man thought it was a good idea too.

Mum went downstairs, but she forgot to bring up a drink of water for Owl, so Billy had to go down and get it. Then he had to go down *again*, to get another for Woggly Man.

'We're not having this every night, Billy,' said Mum, and she carried him upstairs again, and tucked him in.

'Mum,' said Billy.

'Yes?' said Mum.

'Maybe I shouldn't go to school either,' said Billy. 'Maybe I should stay at home with Owl and Woggly Man. That's what Owl thinks.'

'But you liked it!' Mum said. 'You know you did. You liked Ann, and Sam, and Miss Murphy, and all the things to play with, didn't you?'

'Owl *wants* me to stay at home,' said Billy. 'He wants somebody real to play with, not just Woggly Man.'

Mum thought about it.

'I think I know who Owl would like to play with, Billy,' Mum said.

'Who?' said Billy.

And Mum told him.

Next morning, when Billy was getting ready for School, he put Owl and Woggly Man in a carrier bag, and when Billy and Mum were going past the Spaceman's house they put the

carrier bag in the porch, where the Spaceman would be bound to see it.

'I hope they'll be all right, Mum,' Billy said.

'Of course they will,' said Mum. 'Owl and Woggly Man and the Spaceman will all play together, and then none of them will be lonely.'

'But they'll all miss me, won't they?' said Billy.

'Of course they will,' said Mum. 'But you'll see them when you get home!'

Owl and Woggly Man and the Spaceman were all in the Spaceman's garden when Billy got home, and Billy jumped over the Spaceman's wall and joined them.

'We're having a Billy-Getting-Home-From-School-Picnic!' the Spaceman said.

'Can we have one every day?' Billy asked.

'So long as it isn't wet, Billy,' Mum said, looking over the fence.

'Wait a minute,' said the Spaceman. 'Wait. I'm getting a Message. And the Message says:

IF IT IS WET YOU CAN HAVE YOUR PICNIC INSIDE.'

Owl thought that was a great idea.

They had crisps and sweets and apples and fizzy lemonade, and they ate it all up.

'Mum,' said Billy, when Mum was putting him to bed. 'I like school, Mum.'

'Good,' said Mum.

'And Owl and Woggly Man like playing with the Spaceman,' said Billy.

'I'm sure he likes having them,' said Mum.

'So he won't be lonely,' said Billy.

'That's right,' said Mum.

'Good,' said Billy, and he curled up warm and snug under the blankets, with Owl under one arm and Woggly Man under the other, and they all went to sleep.

Owl and Billy and the Space Days

A book for the small ones at
St Mary's Boys Primary School, Newcastle

1 *Moonday*

It was Monday morning, but Billy Ogle didn't have to go to school because he had a whole week's half-term break. He stayed in the garden playing with his special friends, Owl and Woggly Man.

They played Watching Ants and Race-track (Billy won because Billy had the tricycle) and Flying (Woggly Man won because he flew highest when Billy threw him) and Kick-the-Bins.

'Billy!' Mum said. 'Stop that!'

'Why?' said Billy.

'Because it makes a dreadful noise!' said Mum.

'Can we have Bin Band instead?' asked

Billy.

'No,' said Mum.

'Owl wants to have a Bin Band,' Billy said.

'Tell Owl it's absolutely forbidden!' said Mum.

So Billy told Owl, and Owl said they should go to Mr Bennet's and have a Bin Band there instead, because Mr Bennet invented Bin Bands. Mr Bennet was always

94

inventing things. He was a Spaceman who lived in the Old Folks, but nobody knew he was a Spaceman except Owl and Billy and Woggly Man and Mum. It was a secret.

They went to Mr Bennet's.

'Hullo, Mr Bennet,' said Billy. 'Owl wants to have a Bin Band at your house, because Mum won't let us at ours.'

'I don't know that I feel up to Bin Bands this morning, Billy,' said Mr Bennet.

'Why not?' said Billy.

Mr Bennet thought for a bit, and then he said. 'Because it's *Moon*day.'

Billy told Owl, and Owl said it wasn't Moonday, it was Monday, so Billy told Mr Bennet.

'It's Monday, the first day of my holiday!' said Billy. 'Saturday and Sunday don't count, because they aren't school days.'

'And *Moon*day is *my* holiday, Billy!' said Mr Bennet.

'Because you're a Spaceman?' asked Billy.

And Mr Bennett went which means 'YES' in Secret Sign Language.

Billy went ![image] which means 'I'LL
HAVE TO THINK ABOUT IT'.

And he sat and thought about it.
'You're on holiday and we're on holiday,'
Billy said.

![image] went Mr Bennet.
'Owl says if we're all on holiday, we can
have a Bin Band together!' said Billy.

![image] went Mr Bennet.

![image] is the Secret Sign for 'NO',
and Owl thought that Mr Bennet had got
mixed up.

'Owl thinks you meant to go '
said Billy, doing it.

'Owl's wrong,' said Mr Bennet. 'Spacemen don't have Bin Bands on Moondays.
On Moondays Spacemen moon-about. That
means they keep very quiet and do nothing,
and see nothing, and think nothing and

96

smoke their pipes.'

'Oh,' said Billy, sounding very disappointed. 'Don't they play with their friends?'

'It depends on how much mooning they can get in early in the day.' said Mr Bennet. 'If they get mooning right up to tea-time, without any interruption at all, *then* they play with their friends.'

'What do they play?' said Billy.

'Moon Games!' said Mr Bennet.

'Owl wants to know what Moon Games *are*,' Billy said.

'Tell Owl to wait and see,' said Mr Bennet, and then he sat down in his chair and filled his pipe and lit it and puffed and closed his eyes.

'Are you mooning?' Billy asked.

'Not properly,' said Mr Bennet.

'Why not?'

'Because people keep asking me questions!' said Mr Bennet.

Billy told Owl, and Owl said he thought they ought to go home and come back after tea for the Moon Games, so they did.

'Mr Bennet's mooning,' Billy told Mum.

'Oh dear,' said Mum. 'Is he all right?'

'Yes,' said Billy. 'He's keeping quiet and doing nothing and seeing nothing and thinking nothing and smoking his pipe until after tea-time, and then he's playing Moon Games with us.'

'That's very good of him,' said Mum.

'Owl kept asking him questions, and he couldn't moon properly,' said Billy.

'Silly Owl!' said Mum.

'Owl doesn't know what Moon Games are,' said Billy. 'Owl thinks you should go and ask Mr Bennet what Moon Games are, so we'll know if we want to play them. But I told Owl you wouldn't, because that would mean Mr Bennet wouldn't get mooning right up to tea-time!'

'Quite right, Billy,' said Mum, and instead of asking Mr Bennet questions she took Owl and Billy to the swings after lunch, but Woggly Man didn't come because he wanted to moon. He stayed at home in the playbox.

Then they went to the shops and the library and then Mum's hat blew away and Billy got it and then they went home and

Mum and Billy and Owl sat down and mooned.

'Owl's fed up with mooning, Mum,' Billy said. 'He wants to have a Bin Band.'

'A Moonday one?' said Mum.
'What's a Moonday one?' asked Billy.

'One that doesn't make any sound, so it doesn't interrupt all the people who are mooning,' said Mum.

Billy told Owl, but Owl said there was nobody to interrupt, so Billy told Mum.

'Yes there is!' said Mum. 'There's me and Mr Bennet and Woggly Man. We're all mooning up until tea-time, which is why you can only have a Moonday Bin Band.'

So Owl and Billy had a Moonday Bin Band that made hardly any noise at all and then they had a Moonday Tip Toe competition up and down the stairs and then the doorbell went BRIIING-BRIING-BRIING!

Mum stopped mooning, and went to the door.

'Hullo, Mr Bennet,' she said.

'I've come for Owl and Billy,' Mr Bennet said.

'I thought that was *after* tea-time,' Mum said.

'They've been so good letting me moon that I'm inviting them for Moonday tea!' said Mr Bennet. 'You can come too!'

So Mum and Owl and Billy and Woggly

Man all went round to Mr Bennet's for Moonday tea.

They had Moon-biscuits and Moon-burgers and Moon-wine (which was very like orange juice) and then they had Moon Games.

Billy won the Moon Shoot, because he knocked the most Moon-sweets off the chair with the Moon Marble.

Owl won the Moon Hide because no-one could find him when he hid down the sofa.

'I knew where he was, but I didn't tell anybody because I wanted him to win,' Billy said, and Owl let Billy have his Moon-sweet Prize, because Owls don't like sweets.

'It's Moon Treasure time!' said Mr Bennet.

'Oooh!' said Billy. 'What is the Moon Treasure?'

'You'll find out when you find it!' said Mr Bennet. 'First you have to follow the stars.'

'What stars?' said Mum.

But Billy knew what stars, because he'd noticed them when he first came in. They were little yellow stars, grouped together like this,

to make an arrow.

The first arrow pointed out into the hall, and in the hall there was another one, like this,

pointing into the kitchen.

And in the kitchen there was another one like this,

pointing into the cupboard.

And in the cupboard there was a big circle of stars, with the Moon Treasure Box in the middle, like this:

'Shall I open it?' asked Billy, and Mr Bennet said yes. Billy opened the Treasure Box, and it was all filled up with chocolates, wrapped in shiny gold paper, like Moon Pirate doubloons!

Billy ate lots and lots, some for himself, and some for Owl, because Owls get messy with chocolates, and there were still plenty left over to take home for supper time.

'Time to go home now, Billy,' said Mum. 'Say thank you very much to Mr Bennet.'

'Thank you very much, Mr Bennet,' said Billy.

Then Owl whispered something to Billy, and Billy told Mr Bennet.

'Owl says thank you very much too, and can we come and have another Moonday tomorrow?'

Mr Bennet went which means NO.

'Why not?' said Billy.

'Because today is Moonday,' said Mr Bennet. 'Tomorrow is quite a different day.'

'*What* day is it?' demanded Billy.

'Come round to my house tomorrow at two o'clock, and you'll find out!' said Mr Bennet.

'Why two o'clock?' said Billy.

'Wait and see!' said Mr Bennet.

2 *Chooseday*

'Mum,' said Billy. 'Owl wants to know what day it is.'

'Tuesday,' said Mum.

'Not what day it is *here*,' said Billy. 'What day it is at Mr Bennet's.'

'Haven't a clue,' said Mum. 'I can't keep up with these Space Days of Mr Bennet's.'

'Do you think that is what they are?' Billy asked.

'Must be,' said Mum. 'He's a Spaceman, isn't he?'

Owl and Billy and Woggly Man went to Mr Bennet's house, and Billy rang the bell.

'Hullo, Billy,' said Mr Bennet, opening the door.

'It's two o'clock!' Billy said.

'How do you know?' said Mr Bennet. 'You haven't got a watch.'

'I know because I'm *here*,' said Billy. 'You said I had to come at two o'clock and you said it was a special day and you said I would find out what day it was if I came at two.'

'Right!' said Mr Bennet.

'What day is it then?' demanded Billy.

'Twoes-day!' said Mr Bennet. 'On Twoes-day, there is two of everything!' And he took Owl and Billy and Woggly Man inside his house.

'Sit down,' he said, and they sat down.

'Not that way!' said Mr Bennet. 'On Twoesday you have to sit down on two chairs, both at the same time!' and he showed them how to do it.

'Is that all?' Billy said.

'No,' said Mr Bennet. And he showed them how to drink two drinks, both at the same time, with two glasses and two straws. One was lemon and one was orange, and they tasted funny. Then he smoked two pipes, both puffing at the same time, and

making Space smoke rings.

'You try two sweets,' said Mr Bennet.

'I might choke,' said Billy.

'Right!' said Mr Bennet. 'Two sweets, one after the other will do.'

So Billy had two green sweets, and Owl had two yellow sweets, and Woggly Man had two red sweets. Woggly Man and Owl didn't finished theirs, so Billy had to help them.

'Thank you very much for our sweets, Mr

Bennet,' Billy said.

Mr Bennet said that that was all right.

He was only smoking *one* of his two pipes, because he said he hadn't enough puff to keep the two going at once, even though it was Twoesday, so he smoked them one at a time, changing pipes between puffs.

Owl and Billy and Woggly Man sat there watching him do it.

Owl got fed up.

He told Billy about it, and Billy told Mr Bennet.

'Owl doesn't like Twoesday, Mr Bennet,' he said.

'Oh dear!' said Mr Bennet. 'Why not?'

'Because we've got nothing to do,' said Billy. 'Usually when we come to your house there's something to do, but on Twoesday there isn't.'

'I think I'd better check that it *is* Twoesday,' said Mr Bennet. 'Perhaps I got the Space Message wrong.'

They waited and waited and waited for another Space Message to come, while Mr Bennet puffed his pipe.

Then Mr Bennet said, 'The message is

coming. The message says: IT'S CHOOSE-DAY, NOT TWOESDAY!'

'Chooseday?' said Billy. 'What's that?'

'It means *you* choose day,' said Mr Bennet. 'You choose what you want to do.'

Owl and Billy and Woggly Man thought about it. Owl wanted to go to the park and Woggly Man wanted to woggle and Billy wanted to go to Spain.

Billy told Mr Bennet, and Mr Bennet said, '*Choose!*'

Owl and Billy and Woggly Man talked it over, and they decided.

'We choose going to Spain,' said Billy.

'Spain is a long way to walk,' said Mr Bennet. 'Further than the park. I don't know that my legs would take me.'

'You could go on my trike,' said Billy.

'Right across the sea and through France, down to Spain?' said Mr Bennet.

'On your motorbike then,' said Billy.

'I don't think we'd all fit,' said Mr Bennet. 'Better stick to the tricycle.'

'You won't fit on the tricycle,' Billy pointed out.

'But you will,' said Mr Bennet. 'You three

go on the tricycle, and I'll stay here.'

So Owl and Billy and Woggly Man got on the tricycle.

'Which way do I go?' Billy asked.

'Twenty times round the back yard, and then stop at the airport,' said Mr Bennet.

'Where's the airport?' said Billy.

'In the kitchen,' said Mr Bennet.

So Billy and Owl and the Woggly Man went whizz-whizz-whizzing eighteen-nineteen-twenty times round the back yard, and then they stopped and got off the tricycle, and came into the kitchen.

'Buenos dias, Señores!' said Mr Bennet, but Owl didn't know what that meant, until Mr Bennet told him it meant 'Hullo, sirs!' in Spanish, and then Mr Bennet put them on the plane. The plane was two kitchen chairs with a brush laid across for the wings. They got into their seats and Mr Bennet said, 'Los billetes, Señor?' and Owl didn't know what he meant but Mr Bennet told Billy that 'billete' was the Spanish word for ticket, and Billy showed him their tickets.

'Gracias, Señores,' said Mr Bennet. (That means 'Thank you, sirs,' in Spanish.) Then the plane took off and flew all the way to Madrid (which is in Spain), where they were just in time for Spanish tea. Mr Bennet gave Billy el plátano, which was a banana, and el caramelo, which was a toffee, and Billy said 'Gracias' each time, because he was in

Spain. Owl and Woggly Man didn't say it, because they didn't speak Spanish.

Then Billy's mum came.

'Ah! La Señora!' cried Mr Bennet, and he got Billy's mum to show them how to do a Spanish Dance. Then Billy did one too, but Owl and Woggly Man didn't, because they were no good at dancing.

Then Billy's mum said, 'Back to the hacienda!' and they all had to go home, but first they flew back to the airport and then Billy had to trike ride to Mr Bennet's and *then* they went home.

'Hasta la vista! called Mr Bennet, as they went down the road.

'That means "Cheerio till the next time"' said Billy's mum.

'When is the next time?' asked Billy.

'Tomorrow!' said Mum.

Billy thought about it, and then he spoke to Owl, and then he said, 'Yesterday was Moonday, and today is Chooseday *and* Twoes-day, so what day is tomorrow?'

'I don't know,' said Mum.

'I'll go back and ask Mr Bennet,' said Billy.

114

'Oh no you won't,' said Mum. 'You'll have to wait and see!'

3 *Weddingsday*

The next day was Dad's day off so he lay in bed for ages and read his paper, and then he got up and bumped around the house in his old clothes, and then Mum said, 'Time you did the garden!'

'Right!' said Dad, and he had a cup of tea, and then he went out and watered the strawberries, and then he sat down in the deckchair and went to sleep.

'I don't call that doing the garden!' Mum said, looking out of the window.

'Neither do I! said Billy.

'Revenge!' said Mum.

And she got the watering can, and watered Dad!

'Augh!' gasped Dad, as the water sprayed all over him.

'Got you!' said Mum.

Then Dad got the watering can, and he watered Mum.

'What about me?' said Billy.

And they both watered Billy.

'Now we'll all grow like weeds!' said Dad.

Billy watered Owl, because he wanted Owl to grow too.

'Oh Billy!' wailed Mum. 'Poor Owl! He's soaked!' and she pegged Owl up on the line to dry.

'I don't think Owl likes being pegged, Mum,' said Billy, looking at Owl up on the line.

'I'm not sure he liked being watered, Billy,' said Mum. 'Owls don't dry out as quickly as little boys.'

'Is that because Owls are made of pillow-cases, Mum?' said Billy.

'Probably,' said Mum.

'I hope he'll dry out in time for going to Mr Bennet's,' said Billy anxiously.

'I'm not sure you ought to go to Mr Bennet's today, Billy,' said Mum. 'He's a

very old man, and you've been round to play with him a lot. I think he needs another Moonday.'

'With Moon games?' said Billy, hopefully.

'No Moon Games, Billy,' said Mum. 'Just *moon*ing.'

'What's all this about?' said Dad.

So Billy told him about Monday that was Moonday, and Tuesday that was Twoesday and Chooseday.

'And today is Wednesday, but I don't know what Space day it will be,' said Billy. 'That's why I've got to go to Mr Bennet's to find out. This is my holiday, and Mr Bennet said that every day of my holiday was a special day!'

'I think *I* know,' said Dad, suddenly.

'No you don't,' said Billy. He knew Dad didn't, because Dad wasn't a Spaceman, and the Space Days were a Space Secret between Billy and Mum and Owl and Woggly Man, nobody else.

'I do because I'm a very *cunning* dad,' said Dad.

'What day is it then?' demanded Billy.

'It's Weedingsday!' said Dad.

'What do people do on Weedingsday?' asked Billy.

'Weed!' said Dad. 'Weed the garden!' And he got Billy a trowel and a basin and showed Billy the weeds. Billy weeded them.

For ages and ages and ages.

'I've almost run out of weeds, Dad,' Billy said, but Dad didn't say anything. He just lay in the deckchair with his newspaper over his face.

Then Billy saw some big weeds.

They were in the greenhouse.

Billy weeded them.

Billy's dad was cross!

'My tomatoes!' Dad shouted. 'All my lovely tomato plants!' And he rushed up the garden to the greenhouse with Billy's basin, to see if he could replant them.

'What's Dad planting weeds for?' Billy asked Mum.

'Must be for next Weedingsday,' said Mum. 'So you'll have something to weed.' But she told Billy to keep out of Dad's way, just for a while.

'I'll go to Mr Bennet's,' said Billy.

'That might not be such a bad idea,' said Mum, and she unpegged Owl from the line and Billy and Owl went off to Mr Bennet's.

'Good morning, Mr Bennet,' said Billy.

'Good morning,' said Mr Bennet. He was out in his front garden zoom-varooming his motorbike.

'Owl says you should be weeding,' said Billy.

'Why?' said Mr Bennet.

'Because it is Weedingsday!' said Billy, and he told Mr Bennet all about the weeding in the garden, and the extra special big weeds in Dad's greenhouse.

'My dad got very cross,' said Billy. 'But I don't know what about.'

'I think he was cross because he got the day *wrong*, Billy,' said Mr Bennet. 'That's enough to make anyone cross.'

Billy told Owl, and Owl said that Mr Bennet was probably right. Then owl wanted to know what day it really was, and Billy asked Mr Bennet.

Mr Bennet went: which means 'I'll have to think about it'.

'Don't you know?' said Billy.

'I know, but I've forgotten,' said Mr Bennet. 'What day do you think it *might* be?'

Billy asked Owl, and Owl said it might be Owl's day, so Billy told Mr Bennet.

'No, it can't be Owl's day because Space Days sound like earth days, Billy,' said Mr Bennet. '*Moon*day sounds like *Mon*day.'

'And Chooseday sounds like Tuesday!' said Billy.

'What day sounds like Wednesday?' asked Mr Bennet.

'Weedingsday!' said Billy. 'Dad was right, and you were wrong, Mr Bennet. It must be

Weedingsday, because Weedingsday sounds like Wednesday.'

'No it isn't,' said Mr Bennet. 'I got a Space Message about it just before you came, Billy, and the Space Message said: IT ISN'T WEEDINGSDAY: IT'S WED-DINGSDAY.'

'What's Weddingsday?' asked Billy.

'Somebody's getting married!' said Mr Bennet.

'Is it me?' said Billy.

'No,' said Mr Bennet. 'Getting married is for grown-ups.'

Billy told Owl, and Owl said that Mr Bennet had probably got it wrong, just like silly Dad.

'Owl thinks grown-ups getting married isn't much fun,' said Billy. 'He thinks you must have got it wrong.'

'It *might* be fun,' said Mr Bennet.

'How might it be fun?' said Billy.

'It depends who is getting married,' said Mr Bennet. 'If it's someone we know, then we throw things at them and tie things on their cars and shout and cheering and get our photographs taken – So we'd better go and find out who is getting married,' said Mr Bennet.

'Where do we go?' said Billy.

'To the wedding!' said Mr Bennet.

He put on his jacket and Owl and Billy and Mr Bennet got an old boot and some string out of Mr Bennet's spare room and they all went down the road to the shop and Mr Bennet bought a bag of something.

'What's that?' said Billy.

'Confetti!' said Mr Bennet. 'Little bits of coloured paper!'

'What for?' said Billy.

'For throwing all over the someone who is getting married if it is someone we know!' said Mr Bennet. 'If it isn't someone we know, we take it back home again.'

They went down the Main Street, but they didn't see anybody getting married. And there wasn't anybody getting married at the park, either.

Then Mr Bennet saw the car. It was outside a big hotel, and lots of people were running round it tying things onto the back, and squirting it with soap suds.

'That's it!' said Mr Bennet. 'There, where

the Getting Married is going on!'

'The people who are getting married will be very cross when they see their car,' said Billy.

'I don't think they will,' said Mr Bennet, and he took out his string and tied the old boot onto the back of the car, beside lots of other old boots and tin cans and saucepans. 'It's just to make the car look pretty,' he told Billy.

Billy hadn't anything to make the car look pretty with except Owl, so he put Owl in Mr Bennet's boot, but he didn't tell Mr Bennet because Mr Bennet was busy talking to some ladies in big hats who had come out of the hotel.

Then the hotel doors opened.

Miss Murphy came out of the hotel, with Mr Monk. Miss Murphy was Billy's teacher, and Mr Monk was P3's teacher, but they didn't look like teachers. They were all dressed up.

All the ladies in big hats charged! They started throwing confetti at the two teachers!

'Can I throw some?' Billy said.

'Yes,' said Mr Bennet.

And Billy went right up to Miss Murphy and threw his confetti over her.

'Hullo, Billy dear!' said Miss Murphy. And she kissed Billy.

'Atta boy, Billy!' said Mr Monk.

'Are you marrying Miss Murphy?' Billy asked him, because he was worried about wasting his confetti if it was someone else.

'Yes!' said Mr Monk, happily.

'Why?' said Billy.

'Because I love her!' said Mr Monk, and all the ladies cheered and Billy got his photograph taken and everybody shouted and danced about and then Miss Murphy and Mr Monk got into the car which was covered in things and the car drove away.

'What's the matter, Billy?' said Mr Bennet. 'You got your photo taken and you threw your confetti and . . . where's Owl?'

And Billy told him.

'Oh dear!' said Mr Bennet.

'I thought Owl would make the car look pretty,' said Billy. 'I didn't know they were going to drive it!'

'Well, I'm afraid Owl's gone now, Billy,' said Mr Bennet.

'Don't worry,' said Billy. 'Miss Murphy knows Owl. She'll bring him back.

'I *hope* she will, Billy,' said Mr Bennet.

'Miss Murphy always brings Owl back when I leave him places,' said Billy.

'But maybe not on her wedding day,' said

Mr Bennet.

'Why not?'

'Because she'll have lots and lots of things to do and people to talk to, Billy,' said Mr. Bennet. 'She'll be rushing about all over the place, and she might not notice Owl.'

'Oh,' said Billy.

'Let's just hope she will,' said Mr Bennet.

And they both went sadly home.

'Owl's gone on honeymoon!' Mr Bennet told Mum, and Mum took Billy on her knee and said how sorry she was.

'Miss Murphy will bring Owl back!' said Billy.

'Maybe she *won't*, this time, Billy,' said Mum. 'Miss Murphy will be very busy and she might not notice Owl. She might just throw Mr Bennet's old boot away when they clean the car, without looking to see if Owl is inside it.'

'She *will* notice!' said Billy. 'I know, because she's my teacher!'

Then he went upstairs to his room and told Woggly Man about it, and they sat at the window and watched for Owl to come and then . . .

Purrrrrr.

A big taxi came down Billy's street, and stopped outside Billy's door.

'It's Miss Murphy!' Billy shouted.

But it wasn't.

It was Miss Redmond, the headmistress at Billy's school.

Miss Redmond rang the doorbell, and Mum and Billy and Woggly Man answered the door.

'Good afternoon,' Miss Redmond said. 'I believe this boot belongs to Billy.'

And she handed Billy the boot, with Owl inside it.

Billy took Owl out and then he gave the boot back to Miss Redmond.

'Owl belongs to me, but the boot doesn't!' Billy said. 'The boot belongs to Mr Bennet.'

'Oh dear!' said Miss Redmond. 'Miss Murphy said you were to have it specially, Billy, because she's sent you a surprise inside it!'

And there was. In the boot, tied up in a pretty box, was a piece of white wedding cake from Miss Murphy's wedding.

Owl and Billy and Woggly Man had it for their tea.

'Did you enjoy Weddingsday, Billy?' asked Mum, when she was putting him to bed.

'Bits of it,' said Billy, and he told her

about the confetti and getting his photograph taken.

'And the cake,' said Mum. 'And getting Owl back.'

'Y-e-s,' said Billy.

'And Miss Murphy getting married,' said Billy's mum.

'Y-e-s,' said Billy. 'But Owl says Miss Murphy might not come back and teach me any more, now she's got married.'

'Tell Owl he's silly!' said Mum.

And Billy went to sleep remembering all the nice things about Weddingsday, and wondering what the next Space day would be.

4 *Fairsday*

'Mum,' said Billy the next morning, when they were out at the shops, 'What day is it today?'

'Thursday,' said Mum.

'What *Space* Day?' asked Billy.

'No idea, Billy,' said Mum.

'Space days *sound* like ordinary days,' Billy said. 'So it must be a day that sounds like Thursday.'

'GRRRSday!' said Mum, quickly, and she gave a dreadful grrr like a lion.

It made Owl jump.

'You scared Owl!' Billy said. 'Do it again!'

'GRRRR!' went Mum, and she scared the postman, who was going past on his bicycle.

He almost fell off.

'That was a *big* GRRRRR!' Billy said.

'You do one,' said Mum, and Billy went GRRRRRRRR!

Owl said it waas a better GRRRR than Mum's, but Billy didn't tell her.

When Billy got home he did his GRRRRR for Woggly Man, and he GRRRRR-ed through the window at Mrs Wilkins and then he wanted to go and GRRRRR at the

Wilkins' baby, but Mum said he wasn't to because the Wilkins' baby might be scared.

'Like Owl,' said Billy.

'Owl's not a baby,' said Mum. 'Owl wouldn't cry, and be frightened. Wilkins' baby might. You wouldn't want to scare a little baby, would you?'

Billy thought about it. He didn't like the Wilkins' baby much, because it was a boring baby. It couldn't even crawl properly. But he didn't want to frighten it either.

'I don't think it is GRRRRsday anyway, Billy,' said Mum. 'I don't think I would like GRRRRsday, anymore than the Wilkins' baby would. I think it is probably PURRS-day!'

Billy thought about it, and then he asked Owl, and Owl said it might be.

'Do one!' Billy said to Mum. 'Do a purr!'

'I'm not very good at purrs, Billy,' Mum said, but she tried it just the same.

'PURRRRRR!' went Mum.

'GRRRRRing's more fun!' said Billy, and he went off with Owl to practise his GRRRRR so that it would be a better GRRRRR than Mum's.

GRRRRRRR! Billy went to the gate-post and
GRRRRRRRRR! Billy went to Henny's wheelchair, which was outside Henny's house without Henny in it
and

GRRRRRRRRRRRRR! Billy went to Mr Bennet, at his house.

'What are you GRRRRRing for, Billy?' Mr Bennet said.

'I'm GRRRRRing because it is

135

GRRRRRsday!' said Billy.

And Mr Bennet went

'Is it PURRSday?' Billy said.

Mr Bennett went

'What day is it?' asked Billy, impatiently.

 went Mr Bennet.

'Forgotten again?' said Billy.

 went Mr Bennet.

'What about a Space Message?' said Billy, hopefully. 'Owl thinks you should get a Space Message about it.'

'I think Owl is right,' said Mr Bennet. And he sat and thought and thought for a long time in his deckchair.

'How about FURSday?' he said, at last.

'Was that a Space Message?' Billy asked. Fursday didn't sound much fun. It would just be stroking cats and Billy didn't like cats much. Neither did Woggly Man, because Wilkins' cat often sat on him when he was out in the garden.

 went Mr Bennet.

'Wait for the message then,' said Billy.

'I think the Messages are *stuck*, Billy,' said Mr Bennet.

'Space Messages are never stuck,' said Billy.

'This one is,' said Mr Bennet. 'I haven't a clue what day it is. If it isn't GRRRRRsday or PURRsday or FURSday . . . how about HERSday?'

'What do you do on Hersday?' said Billy.

'You do what your mother tells you to, Billy,' said Mum, walking up behind him. 'And that means coming home for your lunch.'

'Will you be able to unstick the message without me?' Billy asked anxiously.

'I'll try,' said Mr Bennet.

'Try very hard,' said Mum.

Billy was just finishing his lunch when Mr Bennet came rushing in. 'I've unstuck the message, Billy!' he said. 'It's a Special Surprise, and we've got to hurry.'

'Can Owl come too?' asked Billy.

'Owl can come,' said Mr Bennet. 'But Woggly Man had better stay at home this time, because we might have our arms full coming back!'

'Back from where?' asked Mum.

'That's a secret!' said Mr Bennet, and he went off with Owl and Billy. They had to go down the street and then they had to go on the bus and then they had to get off the bus and get on *another* bus.

Billy sat upstairs in the second bus, and they got the front seat. Billy drove all the way to the Common, and he TOOTED and PEEPED just like the bus driver down below, and Billy didn't run over anyone.

'Owl wants us to go faster!' Billy told Mr Bennet.

'We can't go any faster than the bus,' said Mr Bennet.

Then they got off the bus and . . .

'I know what day it is!' shouted Billy. 'It's FAIRSDAY!

And it was!

Billy and Owl and Mr Bennet went on the dodgems, and Billy drove, and Mr Bennet got *bumped*.

Then they went on the helter-skelter. Mr Bennet sat down first and Billy sat on Mr Bennet and Owl sat on Billy and Mr Bennet got *banged*, landing on the mat.

They went on a roundabout, and Mr Bennet got *dizzy*, but Billy didn't.

Then Mr Bennet sat down, and Owl and Billy went on the rocket shoot and the

roundabout and the flying horses and the dodgems again, twice (Billy drove and Owl got bumped) and then the swings and then the *giant* slide and then the bouncy castle.

'You come on too,' Billy said to Mr Bennet, and Mr Bennet said, 'I've been bumped and banged and I'm not going to be bounced!'

He didn't go on.

But Billy did, three times.

Owl only went on the first time. He didn't go the second time and the third time because he had been bumped *and* banged *and* bounced, and he wanted to keep Mr Bennet company.

They got ice-creams, and balloons and 'I've been to the Fair' hats and a squeaker and they went home on the bus, and Billy squeaked all the way and then he ran into his own house and he SQUEEEAKED so loudly that Mum almost dropped her cup of tea.

She GRRRRed at Billy.

And Billy SQUEEEEAKED back:

SQUEEAK! SQUEEEAK! SQUEEEAK!

'That's enough, Billy!' said Mum.

SQUEEEAK! went Billy, one last time, and then he stopped.

'Where's Mr Bennet?' said Mum.

'Gone home!' said Billy, and he told Mum all about Mr Bennet being bumped and banged and not bounced and about driving the bus and going on the helter-skelter and the roundabout and the flying horses and the dodgems (three times) and the swings and the giant slide and the bouncy castle, and he showed her his 'I've been to the Fair' hat and his squeaker, but he couldn't show her his ice-cream, because the bit that hadn't melted was inside him, and the bit that had was all over his T-shirt.

'It was a chocky one, Mum,' Billy said.

'I can *see* that, Billy,' said Mum, looking at Owl, who had got a bit chocky-looking himself. 'You know what I think? I think we both ought to go straight round to Mr Bennet's and thank him very much for giving you such a lovely Fairsday.'

And they did.

They rang Mr Bennet's door, but he didn't answer.

He didn't answer, because he was fast asleep in his big chair, in his 'I've been to the Fair' hat.

They could see him through the window, but Mum said not to bang it and wake him up.

'Must be Snoozeday now, Billy!' she said.

And Owl said it must be Snoresday.

They were both right, even though it didn't sound like Thursday at all!

5 *Pieday*

The next morning Mum wouldn't let Billy
go round to Mr Bennet's.

'Mr Bennet played with you on Monday
and Tuesday and Wednesday and Thursday, Billy,' said Mum. 'I expect he needs a
bit of a rest.'

'He had a rest yesterday,' said Billy, remembering Snoresday.

'He's not as young as he used to be, Billy.'

'Then I'll never know what Space Day it
is!' said Billy.

'Yes you will,' said Mum, firmly. 'I think
I know. It is Myday! And on Myday we
have a nice quiet day at home, and don't
bother Mr Bennet.'

'What do we have a nice quiet day *doing*?' asked Billy.

'You can help me with the dishes for a start!' Mum said.

'Owl doesn't want to help with the dishes,' Billy said.

'Nobody asked Owl,' said Mum. 'I'm asking you.'

Billy helped with the dishes, but it went a bit wrong, because Billy decided to show Owl how to blow bubbles with soap suds.

Billy's bubbles floated all over the kitchen, and they popped and popped and popped, popping soap suds over everything.

Mum had to clean all the soap suds up.

Billy and Owl and Woggly Man went out to the garden while she was doing it, to have a nice quiet football match.

C-R-A-S-H! went the cucumber frame.

'Billy!' Mum shouted.

'It was Owl,' Billy said, but Mum didn't believe him.

She didn't believe him about the broken roses either, although Billy told her it was the ball that broke the roses.

'They were goalposts, Mum,' he said. 'We had to have goalposts.'

'Oh, go into the house and keep out of my way, Billy,' said Mum. 'Play something *quietly*.'

So Owl and Billy played throwing Woggly Man down the stairs, *quietly*.

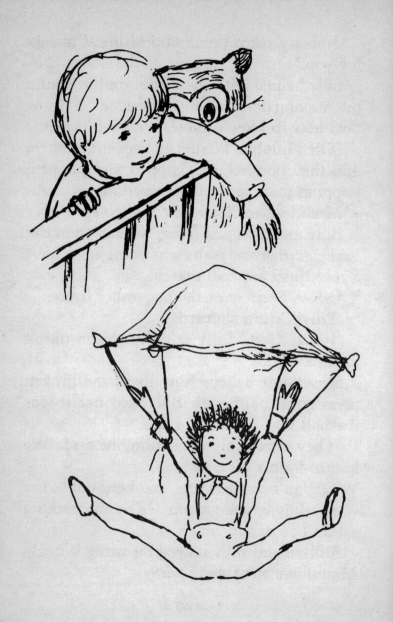

It was a great game. They threw Woggly Man right from the top of the stairs, with Billy's handkerchief tied on for a parachute.

The fourth time Billy missed.

S-M-A-S-H!

'Oh Billy!' said Mum, looking at the smashed flower bowl, with Woggly Man in the middle of it, and the water dripping all over the table.

'That was Woggly Man, Mum,' said Billy. 'He didn't fly straight.'

While Mum was clearing up, Billy gave Owl a nice quiet bath.

Things got *quietly* wet.

Then Billy cleaned the water up with the brush. It was the yard brush, and it made the carpet sort of streaky, because Billy had used it on the garden to flatten out the football pitch.

'Oh *no!*' wailed Mum, when she saw the carpet. 'This just isn't my day!'

'I didn't think it was,' said Billy.

'Go downstairs and sit and DON'T MOVE!' said Mum.

Billy went downstairs and sat and didn't move, but he thought.

When Mum came downstairs again, Billy said, 'I think it must be Cryday, Mum.'

'Cryday doesn't sound very nice, Billy,' said Mum. 'I haven't been as cross as all that, have I?'

'You were a bit,' said Billy, and Mum hugged him.

'It certainly *isn't* Cryday, Billy,' she said. 'But it can't be Myday either. It must be some other day. How exactly does this Space Message thing work?'

'Mr Bennet gets them,' said Billy. 'He sits down and closes his eyes and smokes his pipe for ages and ages and then he gets a message.'

'Let me try,' said Mum.

'You haven't got a pipe,' said Billy.

'I'll try without one,' said Mum.

And she sat and thought and thought and thought, and thought and thought and thought and . . .

'GOT IT!' she said. 'I was wrong. It isn't Myday!'

'What day is it then?' said Billy.

'A day that sounds just like Myday, but isn't,' said Mum. And she told Billy what day it really was.

'Can I do it?' Billy said.

'We'll do it together!' said Mum.

Then she took Billy into the kitchen and
she got out a rolling pin and some flour and
made some pastry and let Billy roll it. She
got a dish and put the pastry in it and then she
sent Billy out to the garden for apples. Mum
got some sugar and she peeled the apples

and she put in the sugar and some other things and popped the whole lot in the oven.

'When will it be ready, Mum?' Billy asked.

'Just in time for Mr Bennet's tea, Billy!' said Mum. 'Can I take it round to him?' Billy asked, and Mum said he could.

And so . . .

just at Mr Bennet's tea-time . . .

his doorbell went . . .

BRINNG! BRINNG! BRINNG!

And Mr Bennet opened the door.

'Hullo, Billy!', he said.

'Hullo, Mr Bennet,' said Billy. 'I bet you don't know what day it is.'

'Friday,' said Mr Bennet.

'It's not Friday,' said Billy. 'It's PIEDAY! and here it is!'

And he gave Mr Bennet the Great Ginormous Apple Pie they had made for his tea.

'Mum said to thank you very much for everything and here's your pie for Pieday!' said Billy, and then he added, looking at the pie, 'I don't think she would mind if you gave a bit to Owl.'

'And you?' said Mr Bennet.

'And me,' said Billy.

They had an Apple Pie Feast and Billy told Mr Bennet about Mum getting Myday wrong.

'She says you're not as young as you used to be,' said Billy.

'Is that so?' said Mr Bennet.

'Yes,' said Billy. 'You need to sleep a lot and you snore, like this!'

And he made a Mr Bennet snoring noise, left over from Snoresday.

'I don't!' said Mr Bennet.

'You do,' said Billy.

'Hmmph!' said Mr Bennet, but he wasn't really cross, because he gave Billy and Owl some more of his sweets before he sent them back to thank Mum very much for a lovely Pieday.

6 Sat-on-day

'It's Sat-on-day today, Billy,' said Mr Bennet, firmly. 'Sat-on-day is the day I sit in my chair all day, because I've got to save my strength for Funday.'

'Is Funday tomorrow?' said Billy.

'Yes,' said Mr Bennet.

Billy told Owl and Owl said that Funday sounded great but he wasn't so sure about Sat-on-day, and Sat-on-day was the day it *was*.

'You can have a different day if you want to,' said Mr Bennet. 'But I'm not having it with you. You have my Space permission to think up your own day, instead of Sat-on-day.'

Billy took Owl home to think about it. They thought about it in the garden. They had to think of days that sounded like Saturday but weren't, which is the way you think of Space Days.

First Billy thought it might be Batterday.

So he went and battered the bins until Mum stopped him.

Then Owl thought of Clatterday, and they clattered the bins they'd been battering, because Mum had told them to stop battering, but she hadn't told them to stop clattering.

156

'Billy!' Mum shouted. 'Stop that at once!'

'It's Clatterday!' Billy shouted back, but Mum said he had to stop it just the same.

Then Billy thought of *another* day.

It was Fatterday.

Billy stuffed one of Mum's cushions in his jersey and he went round the house being fat like Miss Henshawe, but Mum said that wasn't very nice because Miss Henshawe couldn't help being fat, she was just built that way.

'Not like you, Mum,' said Billy, and Mum laughed and said it was Flatterday, was it?

'What's Flatterday, Mum?' Billy asked.

'A day when you go round saying nice things about people and flattering them,' said Mum.

So Billy went up to Woggly Man and said, 'What a nice Woggly Man you are!' and then he *flattered* him all over the carpet.

'What are you doing to Woggly Man, Billy?' Mum asked. 'You'll break him.'

'I'm World Boxing Championing and I'm flattering him, like you said,' said Billy. 'He was standing up, but now he's flattered, because I flattered him!'

Mum told Billy that flattering didn't mean flattening people out, it meant saying things about how wonderful they were, whether you believed the things or not.

'That's silly,' said Billy.

'I agree,' said Mum.

'I don't like Flatterday,' said Billy.

'What about Hatterday, then?' said Mum, and she got her rain hat and put it on Billy.

'Owl hasn't got a hat,' said Billy.

'I don't think Owls wear hats, Billy,' said Mum.

Billy asked Owl and Owl said that that was right, but what about Woggly Man?'

'I don't know about Woggly Man,' said Mum. 'I haven't got a hat for him.'

Billy found one. It was a flowerpot.

Then Mum said, 'Let's stop having Space Days, and have something to eat instead.'

And they did.

When they had finished Billy said, 'What day will it be now, Mum?'

'I don't know, Billy,' said Mum.

But Dad did.

He said it was 'Owzaterday!' and he got some stumps and Billy's bat and ball and

they all played cricket in the back garden.
Billy was the bowler and Dad was the bats-
man and Woggly Man was wicket keeper
and Owl was Owl, because Owls don't play
cricket. Every time Dad missed the ball Billy
shouted '*Owzat*!'

It was a long, long game, and everybody was
tired out when it was finished, so they sat on
the rug in the garden and had Natterday.

'Natterday is when you talk a lot,' said
Dad, and Billy nattered and nattered and
nattered.

'Now we're having What's-the-matter-day!' said Dad. 'Whats-the-matter-with-you that makes you keep having funny days?'

'It's Mr Bennet's fault,' said Billy. 'He said I was to think of my own Space Days.'

'Why don't you go and tell him about all the days you've had then, Billy?' said Dad.

And Billy did.

He woke Mr Bennet up in the garden and he told him about Batterday and Clatterday and Fatterday – which didn't mean flattening people – and Hatterday and Owzaterday and Natterday and What's-the-Matter-day.

'They all *must* be Space Days, because they sound like Saturday,' said Billy.

'The real Space Day is Sat-on-day!' said Mr Bennet. 'I know, because I've been having it, all day!'

'Did you enjoy it?' Billy asked.

'Yes!' said Mr Bennet.

'Then it must be right!' said Billy, and Owl said he thought so too.

7 *Funday*

The next day was Sunday, the very last day of Billy's holidays before he went back to school.

'It's Funday!' he told Mum. 'Mr Bennet says so.'

Mum thought about it. Then she said, 'Fun for who?'

'For me and Owl and Woggly Man and Mr Bennet,' said Billy. 'Mr Bennet sat in his chair all day yesterday and he said we'd have Funday today to make up for it!'

'I suppose he knows what he's doing!' Mum said, but she wouldn't let Billy go round to Mr Bennet's until after lunchtime.

'Hullo, Mr Bennet,' Billy said, when Mr

Bennet opened the door. 'Today's Funday!'

 went Mr Bennet.

'Owl wants to know what we're doing on Funday, Mr Bennet?' Billy said.

And Mr Bennet went

'I thought you'd have already thought about it!' said Billy. 'You had all Sat-on-day to think about it, sitting on your bottom.'

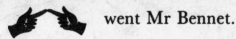 went Mr Bennet.

'What were you doing on Sat-on-day then?' Billy demanded.

'Sitting on my bottom,' said Mr Bennet. 'That's what Sat-on-days are for.'

'We want to know about Fundays!' said Billy.

And Mr Bennet went again.

'All right!' said Billy. '*Do* it!'

And Mr Bennet sat down and thought

and thought and thought for a long, long time and then he said, 'Hold on, I'm getting a message!'

Owl told Billy to stop Mr Bennet getting a message, in case the message said it wasn't Funday after all, and Mr Bennet had got the days mixed up again.

Billy told Mr Bennet, and Mr Bennet

166

said, 'It's not that sort of message. It's a
what sort of Funday is it sort of message and
the message says: S A U S A G E S!'

'Sausages?' said Billy, and he told Owl.

'Owl thinks that that's a funny message,
Mr Bennet,' said Billy.

'There's another bit coming, Billy,' said
Mr Bennet, puffing slowly on his pipe. 'It
says: T I D D L E R S!'

'Does that mean little sausages?' said
Billy.

 went Mr Bennet.

And then he got more of the message.
The next bit said: TENT.

'Sausages, tiddlers and tent?' said Mr
Bennet. 'What does that mean? Do you
know?'

And Billy went (which
means no) because he didn't.

'Hold on!' said Mr Bennet. 'Two more
bits are coming. One says, BACK FIELD
and the other says RIVER.'

'What does that mean?' said Billy.

'Haven't a clue!' said Mr Bennet. 'We'd better ask your mum.'

So they went down to Billy's house.

'We've got a Space Message and we don't know what it means,' Mr Bennet told her.

'It was Sausages-Tiddlers-Tent-Back Field and River, Mum,' said Billy.

'We thought you might know what it means,' said Mr Bennet.

'I think I *do*!' said Mum.

And she sent Billy rushing up the stairs to get Dad's tent from the spare room. Then she got some sausages from the fridge, and Billy's pond net from Billy's room and she put her jeans on and then she said, 'Off we go!'

'Where to?' said Billy.

'The back field, by the river!' said Mum.

And off they all went.

When they got to the river, Billy and Mr Bennet put up Dad's tent and then Billy and Mr Bennet went into the wood and they brought some old sticks and Mr Bennet made a fireplace and Mum said, 'Right! Now we cook the sausages!'

'What in?' said Billy.

'The frying pan,' said Mum.

But they hadn't brought the frying pan with them, because Mr Bennet's message didn't say anything about frying pans. It said: Sausages-Tiddlers-Tent-Back Field and River.

'Your message was wrong, Mr Bennet!' said Billy.

'Oh no it wasn't, Billy,' said Mr Bennet, and he got two forks from Dad's tent pack and he showed Billy how to cook sausages without a pan.

Mr Bennet got very hot in the face, and Billy got very smoky and Mum burnt her finger, but the sausages were brilliant.

'Now! Tiddlers!' said Mr Bennet.

And Billy and Mr Bennet fished for tiddlers in the river.

Owl and Mum and Woggly Man watched, because Owls and Mums and Woggly Men aren't very good at catching tiddlers.

Billy and Mr Bennet went SPLASH!

And SPLOSH!

But they didn't catch a single tiddler.

'I don't think you're doing that the right way!' Mum said, and she rolled up her jeans and went into the river with Billy, and Mr Bennet went to talk to Owl and Woggly Man and smoke his pipe.

Mum crept up on the tiddlers, like this:

And then when they swam into the net she went like this:

And she caught . . .
LOTS!

'Brilliant!' said Billy. 'Catch some more!'
Mum caught some more. Then she
showed Billy how to do it and Billy caught
some and then Mum wanted another go and
she stepped on a big stone and
S P L O O O S H !

'Ooaah!' wailed Mum. 'Help!'
Billy saved her.
'What happened?' Mr Bennet said, wak-
ing up.

'The tiddlers caught *me*!' said Mum.

Then Billy took Woggly Man for a paddle while Mum dried out and then Mum and Billy put the tiddlers back into the water so that they could grow up to be fish. Billy helped Mr Bennet to clear up the fire with water and stones, so that the wind wouldn't light the flames after they'd gone and set all the bushes on fire. Then they packed up Dad's tent and started home.

Owl and Billy and Woggly Man talked all the way home, *natter-natter-natter*!

And Mr Bennet smoked his pipe all the way home, *puff-puff-puff*.

And Mum went *squealch-squealch-squealch* all the way home, because she was still wet.

She squealched right into the kitchen, and she squealched Dad when he laughed at her.

'I can see that you all enjoyed yourselves!' said Dad, and Billy said, 'It was the best Funday ever!'

'And the day after Funday is Schoolday!' said Mum. 'No more Space Days until you get your next holidays!'

Billy thought about it. 'Space Days are more fun than Schooldays, Mum,' he said. 'I

wish there could be Space Days always.'

'Tell that to Mr Bennet!' said Mum.

'I'd like to *be* Mr Bennet,' said Billy. 'Mr Bennet makes fun happen for other people, doesn't he? Like me and Owl and Woggly Man.'

'And me!' said Mum.

'He's a very special old man,' said Dad.

'He's a Spa . . .' Billy began, but then he stopped. Dad didn't know about Mr Bennet, and Billy wasn't going to tell him.

It was a Space Secret between Mr Bennet and Billy and Mum and Owl and Woggly Man, and Billy knew how to keep Space Secrets.

He went to bed with Owl and Woggly Man, and they talked and talked and talked together about the Space Days, until Mum tucked them up and put the light out, and then Billy went to sleep, and *dreamed* about Space Days instead!

A Selected List of Fiction from Mammoth

While every effort is made to keep prices low, it is sometimes necessary to increase prices at short notice. Mammoth Books reserves the right to show new retail prices on covers which may differ from those previously advertised in the text or elsewhere.

The prices shown below were correct at the time of going to press.

☐	7497 0366 0	**Dilly the Dinosaur**	Tony Bradman	£1.99
☐	7497 0021 1	**Dilly and the Tiger**	Tony Bradman	£1.99
☐	7497 0137 4	**Flat Stanley**	Jeff Brown	£1.99
☐	7497 0048 3	**Friends and Brothers**	Dick King-Smith	£1.99
☐	7497 0054 8	**My Naughty Little Sister**	Dorothy Edwards	£1.99
☐	416 86550 X	**Cat Who Wanted to go Home**	Jill Tomlinson	£1.99
☐	7497 0166 8	**The Witch's Big Toe**	Ralph Wright	£1.99
☐	7497 0218 4	**Lucy Jane at the Ballet**	Susan Hampshire	£2.25
☐	416 03212 5	**I Don't Want To!**	Bel Mooney	£1.99
☐	7497 0030 0	**I Can't Find It!**	Bel Mooney	£1.99
☐	7497 0032 7	**The Bear Who Stood on His Head**	W. J. Corbett	£1.99
☐	416 10362 6	**Owl and Billy**	Martin Waddell	£1.75
☐	416 13822 5	**It's Abigail Again**	Moira Miller	£1.75
☐	7497 0031 9	**King Tubbitum and the Little Cook**	Margaret Ryan	£1.99
☐	7497 0041 6	**The Quiet Pirate**	Andrew Matthews	£1.99
☐	7497 0064 5	**Grump and the Hairy Mammoth**	Derek Sampson	£1.99

All these books are available at your bookshop or newsagent, or can be ordered direct from the publisher. Just tick the titles you want and fill in the form below.

Mandarin Paperbacks, Cash Sales Department, PO Box 11, Falmouth, Cornwall TR10 9EN.

Please send cheque or postal order, no currency, for purchase price quoted and allow the following for postage and packing:

UK   80p for the first book, 20p for each additional book ordered to a maximum charge of £2.00.

BFPO   80p for the first book, 20p for each additional book.

Overseas   £1.50 for the first book, £1.00 for the second and 30p for each additional book
including Eire   thereafter.

NAME (Block letters) ....

ADDRESS ....

....

....